An unsuitable game for girls?

Written by Narinder Dhami

Illustrated by Tiziana Longo

Collins

1 The ban

"Well, the Football Association have finally seen sense, and not before time!" Stan Jones announced with satisfaction. He held up the local newspaper and read the headline aloud, stabbing each word with a finger to make his point. *"Women's Football To Be Banned By The Football Association – FA State The Sport Is Unsuitable For Females."*

"What?" Ruby was so startled, she almost sliced through her finger as well as the carrot she was chopping. She was reluctantly helping her mother prepare meat pie, potatoes and vegetables for dinner, while four of her five brothers lounged around the table, chatting idly with their father. Joe, who was 13, was curled up on the hearth rug in front of the fire, immersed in a library book as usual.

"You heard me, Miss," Stan replied, glancing at his daughter. Ruby never looked particularly neat and tidy. Her pinafore dress was always a little grubby, and her woollen stockings were constantly in holes. And as for Ruby's blazing red hair – the exact same colour as his own – those long, corkscrew curls spiralled wildly in all directions and couldn't be tamed by a hairbrush or ribbons.

It was definitely time for Ruby to become a little more ladylike, Stan decided.

"Listen to this." He shook out the paper and began to read. "Doctor Lydia Forster agrees wholeheartedly with the Football Association," Stan read. "She declares: 'Football is a most unsuitable game for women. Kicking a ball is a dangerous movement for females to perform because it might injure their delicate frames.'"

"But you've always said that lady doctors aren't *real* doctors, Dad," Ruby argued, determined to have her say. "And you told us you wouldn't let a lady doctor anywhere near you, not even if you were dying. So why would you take any notice of one now?"

"That's enough of your cheek, Ruby," her father interrupted sternly. "Children should be seen and not heard!"

He waved the newspaper in her direction. "The Football Association is banning ladies' football, and so am I!" Stan declared. "I don't want to see you playing football with your brothers ever again."

Ruby looked dismayed, while all her brothers except Joe roared with laughter. She opened her mouth to respond, but her father shook his head warningly at her. "And no arguing, Miss Ruby!" he added.

"Take that miserable expression off your face, Ruby," her brother Bob said, with a teasing grin. "You can still cook our dinner when we get home after a game, and wash our muddy clothes."

Ruby pulled a face at him. "You're just annoyed because I scored two goals against you yesterday!" she snapped.

"Ruby," her mother said sternly. "Behave yourself. Look at those carrots! You've sliced them much too thickly."

"Sorry, Ma," Ruby muttered. What did it matter *how* she'd sliced the carrots, she thought, frustrated. They'd get eaten anyway, wouldn't they? She was much more concerned about her father banning her from playing football than a bunch of silly old carrots.

Her mother sighed. "You watch the potatoes, Ruby, and make sure they don't boil over." Taking the knife from her daughter, she began deftly reslicing the carrots into thinner circles. "It's time you concentrated on learning to clean, cook and sew, my girl. I'm sick and tired of forever mending the holes in your clothes."

Hastily, Ruby moved over to the stove where
the potatoes were simmering away in a saucepan of
hot water. She had an enormous rip in one seam of
her pinafore dress that, so far, she'd managed to keep
hidden from her mother's eagle eye.

"I've got a couple of shirts that need buttons sewing
on, Ruby," her brother Will called. "That'll keep you
out of mischief."

There was more uproarious laughter.

"Ruby's terrible at sewing," Joe said matter-of-factly. "She's much better at playing football."

"Ruby won't be playing any more football," Stan stated forcefully. "And that's my last word on the subject." He stared scornfully at Joe's book. "You should play a bit more football yourself, son. Nothing good ever came of reading too much."

Ruby rolled her eyes at Joe, who was her favourite brother. What their father said was law in their home, and usually no one ever dared to defy him.

Nevertheless, it *was* completely unfair, Ruby decided silently. During the Great War, which had ended three years earlier, there hadn't been any men left to play football because they were all fighting overseas, so women's football teams had taken their place.

The women's teams had started playing at grounds owned by the Football Association, and they'd attracted huge audiences. Ruby remembered that the women workers at the local factory had formed their own football team, and now the FA were banning women from their grounds and saying that football wasn't a suitable game for girls. It was outrageous!

"Ruby!" her mother shouted, as water cascaded over the sides of the saucepan. "The potatoes!"

2 A secret game

"What a mess!" Her mother stared in despair at Ruby's ham-fisted attempt to sew a button onto Will's shirt. "Here, give it to me and I'll unpick it."

Relieved, Ruby handed the shirt over. Why couldn't Will sew his own buttons on, anyway? She watched as her mother quickly and skilfully removed the stitches.

"Sewing is utterly boring!" Ruby muttered.

Her mother gazed at her, not unsympathetically. "Try to make an effort, Ruby," she urged. "It would really please your dad."

Ruby nodded gloomily.

"Will you run an errand for me, love?" With a few swift stitches, her mother sewed the button on securely and snipped off the remaining thread. "We need some flour, tea and sugar."

"Yes, Ma." Ruby leapt eagerly to her feet. She had her own secret reasons for longing to escape from the house.

"Remember what your dad said about playing football, Ruby," her mother warned, handing her daughter some coins. "You stay away from the park, now."

"But the park's a short cut to the grocery shop," Ruby protested. "And I can search for wildflowers for my pressed flowers collection."

"I didn't know you had a pressed flowers collection," her mother said suspiciously.

"I don't," Ruby replied, her eyes wide and innocent. "I'm going to start one."

"I'll expect you back here in half an hour," her mother replied. "And don't you dare be late, Miss Ruby, or there'll be trouble."

Shoving the coins into her pinafore pocket, Ruby strolled casually out of the house as her mother watched. Once outside, though, she sprinted as speedily as she could down the street towards the park, hoping her friends May, Lizzie and Dorothy would already be there. Her friends were just as enthusiastic about football as Ruby herself, but so far, their parents hadn't banned them from playing.

To Ruby's delight, she spotted the three girls immediately. May, Dorothy and Lizzie were kicking an old, heavy football around the field, shrieking with laughter. Elated, Ruby rushed over to join them. She'd never really disobeyed her father before, but, Ruby reasoned, what her dad didn't know, couldn't hurt him! She'd just make certain he never discovered what she was up to.

The girls hadn't noticed her, so Ruby sneaked over, launched herself forward and swept the ball off Lizzie's toe, just as she was poised to thwack it to Dorothy.

"Ruby!" Lizzie hollered. "You give that back!"

"Come on, let's have a quick game," Ruby pleaded breathlessly, shielding the ball as Lizzie attempted to tackle her. "I've only got half an hour!" She dummied Lizzie and sent her the wrong way, then booted the ball to May. "I'm supposed to be going to buy groceries."

"What about your dad?" May asked. The girls knew all about Ruby's football ban.

"What about him?" Ruby retorted. "He's safely out of the way at work!"

The girls found some large stones to mark the goalposts, then they split up into two teams, Ruby and May against Lizzie and Dorothy.

Her red curls flying, Ruby was exhilarated as she charged towards the opposition's goal, dribbling the ball neatly in front of her. This was the first time she'd played football for a week. Her brothers had refused to allow her to join in their games anymore because they wouldn't disobey their father. Ruby thrust aside the thought of what her father would say if she got caught. The punishment would be worth it!

Lizzie and Dorothy were racing alongside Ruby, trying to hook the ball away from her. Ruby evaded them both and let loose a thunderbolt of a shot.

"GOAL!" May roared excitedly.

"Ouch!" Ruby groaned, collapsing onto the grass. It had taken a huge amount of effort to whack the heavy ball so hard, and her ankle was now throbbing with pain.

"Are you all right?" someone called, as the other three girls gathered around Ruby with expressions of concern. Gingerly massaging her ankle, Ruby glanced up to see a well-dressed woman coming towards them. It was Doctor Helen Murray. Ruby recognised her straightaway because she was a governor at her school and often visited to talk to the pupils. Ruby also knew that Doctor Murray had just moved into one of the posh houses whose enormous gardens bordered the park.

"She calls herself a doctor," Ruby's father had remarked scornfully. "As if a woman can be a proper doctor!"

"You're a pupil at Summerfield School, aren't you?" Doctor Murray said. "What's your name?"

"Ruby Jones," Ruby replied, wincing a little.

"May I look?" Doctor Murray pointed at Ruby's leg. Ruby nodded, blushing as the doctor knelt beside her and gently probed her ankle. "I don't think you've done any real damage," Doctor Murray said, rising to her feet and brushing grass from her skirt. "Just be careful for the next few hours. No running around."

"Thank you, Doctor Murray," Ruby called, as the doctor walked away. "At least May and I won 1–0! I'd better go to the grocery shop, though, or Ma will be after me."

"And I've got to get home fast, before my brother notices I borrowed his football!" Dorothy said, with a chuckle.

"You mean *this* football?" asked a teasing voice.

A group of older boys was standing laughing at them, one of them clutching the girls' football.

"Football isn't a suitable game for girls!" one of them said.

"So don't try playing football here again, because we'll be waiting for you," another added. Then, still chortling, the boys departed, taking the football with them and leaving four very disgruntled girls behind.

3 The game must go on!

"No." Joe shook his head. "It's a daft idea, Ruby."

"No, it isn't!" Ruby said indignantly. "I can't play football at home, and we can't play in the park either because of those boys. This is the perfect solution!"

Ruby had racked her brains and finally come up with a plan. She'd ask Doctor Helen Murray if she and her friends could play football in the doctor's enormous back garden.

"I don't know why you need me to be involved," Joe grumbled.

"Because otherwise Ma and Dad will be suspicious!" Ruby retorted impatiently. "I pretend I'm going to the library with you, but really I'm playing football in Doctor Murray's garden."

"If she agrees," Joe pointed out.

"Let's go and ask her," Ruby replied.

Ruby was full of determination, but as she
and Joe approached Doctor Murray's house, her
self-confidence began to falter. The house was large
and imposing, with marble steps up to the front door.
Nervously, Ruby paused at the garden gate. Joe, too,
looked apprehensive.

"Have you changed your mind, Ruby?" he
asked hopefully.

Then they heard the sound of footsteps rapidly
approaching from the other end of the street.
Ruby turned – and there was Doctor Murray.

"Hello again," she said, her very direct eyes fixed on Ruby. "How's your ankle?"

"It's fine, thank you," Ruby muttered awkwardly, wishing she was a million miles away. "This is my brother, Joe."

"So why are you here?" Doctor Murray enquired.

Ruby squirmed with embarrassment. Why had she ever thought this was a good idea? "I – I was hoping you'd allow my friends and I to play football in your back garden, please," she muttered.

"I see." Doctor Murray gazed thoughtfully at them. "You'd better come inside. We'll have tea, and you can explain yourselves properly."

Ruby and Joe nudged each other excitedly as Doctor Murray unlocked the door.

"Make yourselves comfortable," Doctor Murray said, as she showed them into a huge living-room, filled with light and furnished with deep, squashy sofas, watercolour paintings in gold frames, and flowers everywhere. "I'll go and ask my maid to bring us tea."

Left alone, Ruby and Joe prowled around, wide-eyed.

"This house is beautiful!" Ruby whispered. Her feet sank into the plush carpet as she padded over to the window. "And look at the back garden – it's perfect!" The garden had lawns and trees, but very little else. There were no flower borders and no vegetable patch.

Joe didn't reply. He'd caught a glimpse of bookshelves through an open door, and he was peeking longingly into the next room. "There are hundreds of books in here, Ruby," he said, eyes shining. "Imagine having a library at home, all to yourself!"

The living-room door opened, and Doctor Murray returned, followed by her maid with a tea tray.

"Now," Doctor Murray said, handing round slices of fruit cake, "explain why you want to play football in my back garden."

Hesitantly, Ruby explained that the girls couldn't play in the park because some of the older boys wouldn't allow it. She said nothing about her father's ban. Doctor Murray was silent for a few moments after Ruby had finished speaking, but she appeared sympathetic.

"And your parents know you're here?" she asked.

"Yes," Ruby replied boldly. Joe shot her a startled look and almost choked on a cake crumb.

"Well – " Doctor Murray replaced her empty teacup on the tray. "I'm hoping to have the garden landscaped soon, because it's rather a mess. But I see no objection to you using it in the meantime. There's nothing to be damaged, as long as you stay at the far end, away from my windows." She smiled. "I think the FA's football ban is ridiculous!"

Ruby grinned. "Oh, thank you, Doctor Murray!" she exclaimed fervently. She could scarcely believe her luck. Against all the odds, she'd still be able to continue playing football!

"And are you a footballer, too?" the doctor asked Joe.

"No, I like reading." Joe's eyes strayed towards the bookshelves in the next room. "I'm just here – er – to look after Ruby."

"Then you're welcome to browse through my library while your sister is playing football," Doctor Murray replied, moving over to the door. She flung it open wider, displaying the packed bookshelves. "I have a variety of books. You're bound to find something that interests you."

Joe was speechless with delight. Ruby grinned and poked him in the ribs with her elbow.

"Manners, Joe!" she whispered. She was certain she wouldn't have any problem at all persuading Joe to accompany her to Doctor Murray's now!

"Thank you, Doctor Murray." Joe just about managed to get the words out.

"Then I'll see you both tomorrow afternoon." Doctor Murray smiled. "More cake?"

4 New ideas

"GOAL!" Ruby hollered, delighted
with herself. She'd just smashed the ball past Dorothy,
the opposition goalkeeper, and now her team were
3–0 up.

"Well done, Ruby," Doctor Murray called
from the patio. She lowered her book to her lap
and applauded. Joe, who was also reading, did
the same.

"Thank you!" Ruby waved and beamed at them.

This was Ruby's third visit to Doctor Murray's garden to play football, and she'd been joined by Lizzie, May, Dorothy and several more of their friends.

Meanwhile, Joe was loving the opportunity to wander around Doctor Murray's library, reading whatever he chose.

And no one at home suspected a thing! Everything had worked out for the best, Ruby thought contentedly. Although she felt guilty at deceiving her parents, Ruby assured herself she wasn't doing any harm.

When the game was over, Ruby dawdled behind
the other girls, waiting for Joe. He was having
a conversation with Doctor Murray on her doorstep.

"What were you talking about?" Ruby asked
curiously when Joe joined her.

"I told Doctor Murray I want to be a teacher,"
Joe replied. "She's going to help me."

"Really?" Ruby gasped. Her brothers were expected
to start work at the same factory as their father after
leaving school.

Ruby smiled enthusiastically. "I can't believe she's a real doctor, *and* she lives in that great big house all alone, without a husband!" she marvelled. "I want to be just like her when I grow up."

Joe was startled. "You want to become a doctor?"

"Yes, why not?" Ruby retorted.

"And what do you think Dad will have to say about that?" Joe asked, raising his eyebrows.

Ruby thumped his shoulder playfully, and they dashed home through the park.

"You two are spending a good deal of time at
the library at the moment," their mother remarked,
as she poured a cup of tea for their father.

Ruby and Joe exchanged glances as their father
snorted with disgust, folding up his newspaper.
"I've told you before, Joe, you spend too much
time with your nose in a book," he said, frowning.
"And Ruby should be at home learning how to
keep house."

"Oh, Stan, leave the children alone while they have their tea," their mother chimed in, pouring herself a cup. "Didn't you borrow any books today, Joe?"

Joe blushed guiltily, tongue-tied.

"He couldn't find anything he liked." Ruby spoke up quickly.

"And did you find anything for your pressed flower collection on your way home through the park, Ruby?" her mother enquired.

"Not this time," Ruby replied, without blushing at all.

"Collecting flowers is a very pleasant pastime for girls," her father said approvingly. "Much more suitable than playing football."

"Sorry, I nearly gave the game away!" Joe whispered to Ruby, when they were on their own a little later. "You know I'm terrible at telling fibs."

"We're not lying *exactly*," Ruby replied. "We're just bending the truth a little, that's all."

The following afternoon, Ruby and Joe hurried up the marble steps towards Doctor Murray's front door, as usual.

"I wonder what we'd do right now if Dad happened to walk past and spot us?" Joe remarked.

Ruby shuddered. "Don't even think it!" she groaned. She'd just rung the doorbell, when they heard a familiar voice behind them.

"And what are you two doing here, when you're supposed to be at the library?"

5 A different kind of future

Ruby and Joe whirled around, faces burning with guilt. Their mother was marching furiously up the steps towards them.

"M-Ma!" Ruby spluttered, her heart sinking. She was heartily relieved that it wasn't their father who'd caught them red-handed, but their mother was bound to tell him …

"I guessed something suspicious was afoot," their mother said grimly. "So I followed the pair of you. What are you doing here, at Doctor Murray's house?"

Ruby and Joe spoke simultaneously.

"Playing football."

"Reading books."

Their mother stared at them in disbelief, as the front door opened.

"Sorry to keep you waiting," Doctor Murray apologised. "I was working, and I forgot it was my maid's day off – " Her voice tailed away as she realised Ruby and Joe weren't alone. "Oh, hello. You're Mrs Jones, aren't you? I've seen you at the school."

"I am," their mother snapped. "And I'd very much like to know what's been going on here!"

Doctor Murray swung the door open wider. "It's a great pleasure to make your acquaintance at last, Mrs Jones," she replied calmly. "Let's go inside where we can talk in private."

In the living room, Ruby and Joe waited in miserable silence, while Doctor Murray explained about Ruby's request to be allowed to play football in her garden.

"I must apologise, Mrs Jones," she concluded. "Obviously, I'd no idea they didn't have your permission."

"Well, they didn't!" Their mother threw Ruby and Joe a reproving glance. "Neither their father nor I knew anything about it."

Ruby and Joe exchanged alarmed looks. If their father got to hear about this … !

"It was very wrong of them to deceive you, Mrs Jones," Doctor Murray replied. "But can I congratulate you on having two remarkable and extremely intelligent children?"

Their mother looked taken aback for a moment, then she smiled proudly.

"Ruby and I have had several discussions about how difficult it can be for girls to achieve our ambitions." For a moment, Doctor Murray looked very downcast. "My own father was completely against me going to university and becoming a doctor."

"My father was exactly the same," Mrs Jones confided sadly. "I was told I had a beautiful voice, and I wanted to take singing lessons. But he refused to allow it."

Ruby and Joe stared at each other, stupefied. They'd *never* heard their mother mention this before. But then Ruby suddenly remembered numerous times when she'd heard her mother singing as she performed routine household tasks like peeling potatoes, scrubbing floors and washing clothes. It was true – Ma *did* possess a beautiful, melodic voice.

"Let's hope things might change in the future," Doctor Murray sighed. "Mrs Jones, Ruby is a lively, bright and courageous girl, and both she and Joe have very promising futures ahead of them, I'm sure. I'd be very happy, if you allowed it, for them to continue visiting me."

"We'll see about that," Mrs Jones replied evasively. "Good afternoon, Doctor Murray."

Ruby and Joe didn't dare speak a word as they accompanied their mother out of Doctor Murray's house. What a disaster, Ruby thought gloomily.

"Don't you two have anything to say for yourselves?" Mrs Jones demanded. "Doctor Murray seems to think very highly of the pair of you. I'm not sure why."

"Ma, you never told us you wanted to be a singer!" Ruby exclaimed.

"Your grandpa forbade me to sing at all," her mother replied. "But I used to sneak off to my friend Josie's house because her dad had a piano and we used to gather around it for a sing-song–" Mrs Jones paused abruptly, looking highly embarrassed.

Ruby and Joe burst into laughter.

"*Please* can we visit Doctor Murray again, Ma?"
Joe asked bravely. "She's going to help me become
a teacher."

"A teacher?" Mrs Jones repeated.

"And I'd like to be a doctor," Ruby added.

To their amazement, Ma began to chuckle. "Oh, I'd
love to see your dad's face when he discovers that!"

"You won't tell Dad I disobeyed him, will you, Ma?"
Ruby asked hopefully.

"Of course I'll be telling him," Mrs Jones said
matter-of-factly.

Ruby and Joe glanced at each other in utter horror.

"But I'll be telling him in my own good time," their mother continued breezily. "I know how to handle your father. You leave him to me!"

"So, can we still visit Doctor Murray?" Joe persisted.

"Yes – but *only* if Ruby learns to bake a cake and sew on a button," their mother stipulated.

"I promise I will," Ruby said earnestly. "But *only* if Joe learns those things, too."

"Me?" Joe exclaimed. "But that's girls' stuff!"

Ruby raised her eyebrows at him.

"Well, all right," Joe agreed reluctantly.

"And maybe sometime in the future, the FA will decide that women should be allowed to play football," Ruby said dreamily. "And then Dad will realise that it *isn't* an unsuitable game for girls!"

Petition to the Football Association

Dear Sirs,

We're extremely disappointed with your recent decision to ban females from playing football on your grounds. We definitely disagree with your statement that football is an unsuitable game for girls! There are many girls and women throughout the country who love playing football and we deserve your support.

We're asking you please to reconsider your decision.

Signed by:

Ruby Jones

Joseph Jones

Mrs Doris Jones

Doctor Helen Murray

May Carter

Dorothy Cohen

Elizabeth Bowen

Jane Barton

Lucy Richards

Maria Reynolds

Jennifer Spratt

Katherine Piper

Vera Mackie

Margaret Lockley

 Ideas for reading

Written by Gill Matthews
Primary Literacy Consultant

Reading objectives:
- check that the book makes sense to them, discussing their understanding and exploring the meaning of words in context
- draw inferences such as inferring characters' feelings, thoughts and motives from their actions, and justify inferences with evidence
- provide reasoned justifications for their views

Spoken language objectives:
- use relevant strategies to build their vocabulary
- articulate and justify answers, arguments and opinions

Curriculum links: Relationships education – Respectful relationships

Interest words: grumbled, retorted, enquired, exclaimed

Resources: IT

Build a context for reading

- Explore the covers of the book, reading the title and back-cover blurb.
- Ask children what they think *unsuitable* and *suitable* mean. Discuss why someone would think girls shouldn't play football.
- Ask what children think *ingenious* means and what Ruby's solution might be.
- Discuss children's experiences of stories with historical settings. How does knowing this is a story set in the past help them to prepare to read it?

Understand and apply reading strategies

- Read pp2–7 aloud using appropriate expression. Ask children what they think about the football ban and Stan's comments. Encourage them to support their responses with reasons.
- Ask children to read pp8–14. Discuss what kind of person the children think Ruby is. What do they think about Stan's comment to Joe?
- Children can read pp15–26. Ask how the events in this chapter have added to their impression of Ruby.
- Give children the opportunity to read the rest of the story.